For Roger, Kay, and Big Bad Sam —L.J.

For Chris, K.Y.A.B. —C.W.

CIP Data is available.

First published in the United States 1993
by Dutton Children's Books,
a division of Penguin Books USA Inc.
375 Hudson Street, New York, New York 10014

Originally published in Great Britain 1993
by Magi Publications, London

Printed in Belgium
First American Edition
ISBN 0-525-45155-2
1 3 5 7 9 10 8 6 4 2

Dutton Children's Books New York

The Dog Who Found Christmas

by **Linda Jennings**

illustrated by **Catherine Walters**

When Buster was a little puppy, he had to leave his mother and go to a new home. At first, his new family petted him and called him cute.

But as Buster grew from a puppy into a little dog, things began to go wrong. He tried his best to please, but his owners yelled at him when he jumped on them or chewed things.

"Bad dog!" they shouted. "You're more trouble than you're worth!"

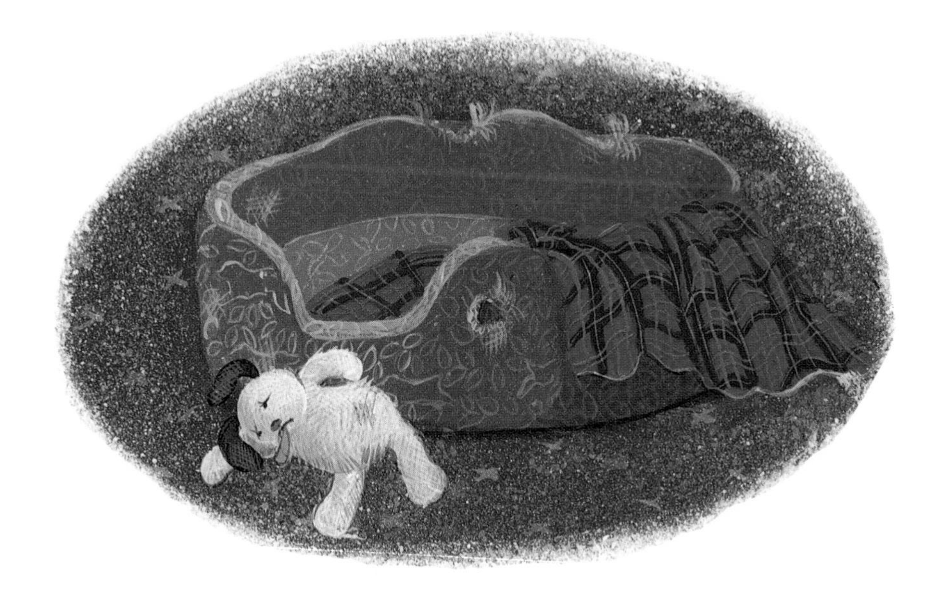

One cold winter's day, his family took Buster to a part of town where he had never been before. They pushed him out of the car and left him on the edge of a wide, busy road.

They didn't want Buster anymore.

The cars raced by all day, but nobody noticed poor Buster. It grew dark, and the car headlights shone like huge, fierce eyes. Buster was very frightened. He wondered why his family didn't come back for him. He wanted to go home, but he didn't know where home was.

Without thinking, Buster rushed out into the road. SCREECH! Two cars swerved to avoid him. The drivers leaned out of their windows and yelled at the little dog.

BRM BRMM

Buster ran into a yard and lay trembling under a bush. He waited and waited. When his heart stopped thumping so loudly, he came out. It was very cold, and he was hungry.

He crept up to the front door of a house and scratched at it. The door opened, and a woman looked down at Buster. But before she could say anything, a huge, snarling dog appeared from behind her and thrust its head into Buster's face.

"Go away, before I bite you!" he growled. "This is *my* home."

Suddenly the big dog broke free and chased Buster down the path, snapping at his short, stumpy tail. Buster just managed to squeeze through a hole in the hedge before the big dog could nip him again.

Buster sat on the frosty pavement, licking his sore tail. He wondered where he should go. He trotted on and hesitated at another open gate. There were lights sparkling on a tree in the window. The house looked very cheerful and welcoming.

Buster started to walk up the driveway, but he didn't get far.

"Scram, you mutt!"

Buster looked up. Sitting on the wall above him was a large tabby cat.

"My territory," he hissed. The cat showed his claws and his sharp, white teeth.

"Okay," sighed Buster, "I'll go."

Nobody wants me, thought Buster.

It started to snow, and Buster's fur grew wetter and wetter. His little body shook with cold.

Some people were walking down the road, singing. Buster thought if he could move along with them, they might notice him and take him home. Keeping his distance, he followed them.

The singers turned into a driveway. "Silent night, holy night," they sang as they stood in a circle outside a house. Buster crept among them, wondering if they would notice him but worrying that if they did, they might tell him to go away.

The door to the house opened, and Buster could smell something delicious. His stomach grumbled with hunger.

"One for each of you," said a voice, and a hand held out a plate of cookies.

"Thank you, Mr. Merriweather," said the carolers.

"And one for the little dog," he added.

"What little dog?" everyone asked. They looked down at their feet. Buster gazed up at them with pleading eyes.

"Who is he? Where did he come from?" the carolers asked.

"He must be a stray. He looks very hungry," said a little girl, and she gave Buster a cookie. He swallowed it in one gulp.

Mr. Merriweather came out of the house and looked at Buster.

"I'll take him," he said. "I think he needs a good home, and I've always wanted a dog for Christmas." He put out his hand to Buster, but the little dog drew back, afraid.

"Come on, little fellow," said Mr. Merriweather gently. "We'll have a good Christmas together, you and I."

Buster stretched contentedly in front of the fire. His tummy was full, and he felt warm at last.

"Welcome home, little dog," said Mr. Merriweather.

"Woof!" said Buster.